THE RED PYRAMID

THE GRAPHIC NOVEL

RICK RIORDAN

Adapted by
ORPHEUS COLLAR

Lettered by
JARED FLETCHER

Disney • Hyperion Books
New York

CHAPTER

1

LONDON.
NOW.

It happened on *Christmas Eve.* My dad and I had just flown into Heathrow Airport after a couple of delays, late to pick up my sister, Sadie, for visitation day.

The whole taxi ride, my dad seemed kind of *nervous.*

I've lived with my father ever since my mom died. He trained me early to keep all my belongings in a single carry-on suitcase.

My dad packed the same way, except he was allowed an extra workbag for his tools.

Dad's an archaeologist, so we're always on the move. Mostly we go to Egypt, since that's his specialty. Go into a bookstore, find a book about Egypt, there's a pretty good chance it was written by Dr. Julius Kane.

It turns out there were other reasons my dad moved around so much, but I didn't know his *secret* back then.

For Sadie, life was different. When Mom died, her parents (our grandparents) had a big court battle with Dad. They blamed him for Mom's death and won the right to keep Sadie with them in England. So I traveled around with Dad, and Sadie was raised as a British schoolkid.

I was only six when our family was separated. My gran and gramps said they couldn't keep us both--at least that was their excuse for not taking **Carter**. Now **Dad** is allowed two visitation days a year--one in summer and one in winter--because my grandparents hate him.

And he was always late!

I don't like waiting.

MROWR...

WHAT'S THAT, **MUFFIN**? YOU SEE THEM?

My cat, Muffin, had been a going-away gift from Dad six years before. But with her attitude, I don't know if I'd call her a proper gift. She was a weird cat who never got bigger or older.

FINALLY.

I CAN'T WAIT TO HEAR WHY THEY'RE LATE *THIS* TIME.

DRIVER, PLEASE WAIT FOR US HERE. WE'LL ONLY BE A MOMENT.

CARTER, GO ON AHEAD.

BUT--

GET YOUR SISTER. I'LL MEET YOU BACK AT THE TAXI.

HOLD DOWN THE FORT, EH?

MROWR

TIME TO GO PRETEND WE'RE A HAPPY FAMILY.

You'd never guess Sadie's my sister. We look nothing alike. When you only see each other twice a year, it's like you're distant cousins rather than siblings. We had absolutely nothing in common except our parents.

Faults 1020

SO IT'S *YOU* AGAIN. THE *JUNIOR PROFESSOR.*

Sadie likes to tell me that I don't have any style.

The boy had never been in a proper school, and he dressed like an old man in his button-down shirt and loafers.

WHERE'S DAD?

ARGUING WITH SOME GUY ACROSS THE STREET.

Maybe she's right. But Dad had drilled into my head that I always had to dress my best.

YOU DON'T KNOW WHO IT IS?

DO WE HAVE TO STOP FOR *EVERY* MONUMENT?

I HAD TO SEE IT AGAIN, WHERE IT HAPPENED...

THE LAST PLACE I SAW YOUR *MOTHER*.

ARE YOU TELLING US SHE DIED HERE? AT CLEOPATRA'S NEEDLE? WHAT HAPPENED?

DAD! I GO PAST THIS EVERY DAY. YOU MEAN TO SAY-- ALL THIS TIME-- I DIDN'T EVEN KNOW?

DO YOU STILL HAVE YOUR CAT?

MUFFIN? OF COURSE I DO! WHAT DOES THAT HAVE TO DO WITH ANYTHING?

AND YOUR *AMULET?* LET ME SEE IT.

Right before we were separated, Dad gave us both Egyptian amulets.

Mine had been Mom's. It looked a bit like an angel, or perhaps a killer alien robot.

Carter's was obviously an *eye.*

The *Eye of Horus,* actually. Dad says it was a popular protection symbol in Ancient Egypt.

HAPPY NOW? BUT DON'T CHANGE THE SUBJECT. GRAN'S ALWAYS SAYING YOU CAUSED MUM'S DEATH. THAT'S NOT *TRUE*, IS IT?

DRIVER, PLEASE CONTINUE TO THE MUSEUM.

LOVELY. OUR PARENTS WERE SECRETLY PAGAN OCCULTISTS WHO WORSHIPPED ANIMAL-HEADED GODS.

NOT WORSHIPPED. BY THE END OF THE ANCIENT TIMES, EGYPTIANS HAD LEARNED THAT THEIR GODS WERE NOT TO BE WORSHIPPED. THEY ARE POWERFUL, PRIMEVAL FORCES, BUT THEY ARE NOT DIVINE IN THE SENSE ONE MIGHT THINK OF *GOD*.

THEY ARE CREATED ENTITIES, LIKE MORTALS. WE CAN RESPECT AND FEAR THEM, *USE THEIR POWER*, OR, IF NECESSARY, *FIGHT* THEM--

--BUT WE DON'T WORSHIP THEM. THOTH TAUGHT US THAT.

IT'S GETTING LATE. IF YOU'RE GOING TO SURVIVE AND SAVE YOUR FATHER, YOU HAVE TO GET SOME REST.

SORRY, DID YOU SAY SURVIVE AND SAVE OUR FATHER?

MUCH OF WHAT WE HAVE TO SPEAK ABOUT IS BETTER DISCUSSED IN DAYLIGHT. YOU NEED SLEEP, AND I DON'T WANT YOU TO HAVE NIGHTMARES.

YOU THINK I CAN SLEEP?

KHUFU!

AGH!

Khufu led Sadie and me to adjoining rooms on the third floor, and I have to admit, they were way cooler than anyplace I'd ever stayed before.

All my favorite snacks, a comfortable shower, enormous beds, fresh pj's, a view of Manhattan--

But we were locked in! Something felt wrong.

CARTER?

YES, SADIE.

DO YOU THINK AMOS... I MEAN, CAN WE TRUST HIM?

IF AMOS WANTED TO HURT US, HE COULD'VE DONE IT BY NOW. TRY TO GET SOME SLEEP.

IT REALLY **WAS** MAGIC, WASN'T IT? WHAT HAPPENED TO DAD AT THE MUSEUM. AMOS'S BOAT. THIS HOUSE. ALL OF IT'S **MAGIC.**

I THINK SO.

GOOD. AT LEAST I'M NOT GOING MAD.

I MISS DAD. I HARDLY EVER SAW HIM, I KNOW, BUT... I MISS HIM.

My eyes got a little teary, but I took a deep breath.

I had to be stronger. Sadie needed me. Dad needed us.

WE'LL FIND HIM.

CHAPTER

2

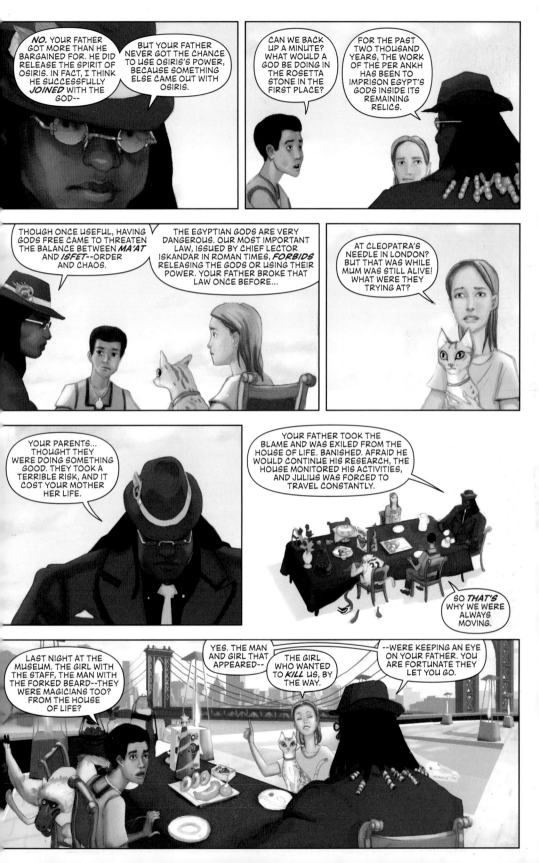

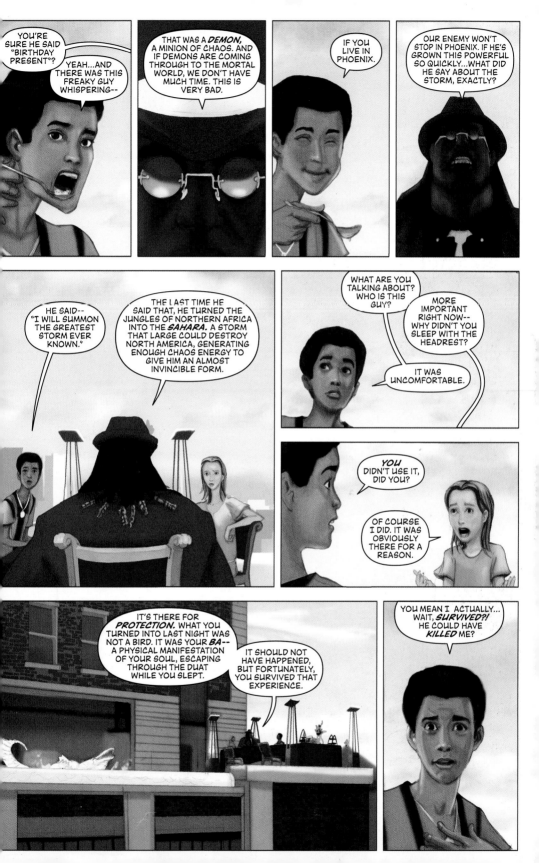

Go away! I'm not a mouse!

WHAT *ARE* YOU?

I'm a *shabti,* of course! Master calls me Doughboy, though I find the name insulting.

You may call me supreme-force-who-crushes-his-enemies!

DOUGHBOY, THE MASTER IS OUR DAD, AND HE'S MISSING. HE'S BEEN MAGICALLY SENT AWAY SOMEHOW AND WE NEED YOUR HELP--

Master is *gone*?

HA-HA! Free at last! See you, suckers!

FREE! FREE!

Trapped! Trapped!

OH, SHUT UP. I'M THE MISTRESS NOW. AND YOU'LL ANSWER MY QUESTIONS.

NOW, DOUGHBOY, FIRST OFF, WHAT'S A SHABTI?

"Shabti" means *answerer,* as even the stupidest slave could tell you.

THE EGYPTIANS MADE MODELS OUT OF WAX OR CLAY--SERVANTS TO DO EVERY KIND OF JOB THEY COULD IMAGINE IN THE AFTERLIFE.

But afterlife work is only one use for shabti. We are used for a great number of things in *this life,* because magicians would be total incompetents without us doing the hard work!

HMM. WHY DID DAD CUT OFF YOUR LEGS BUT LEAVE YOU WITH A MOUTH?

He cut my legs off so I wouldn't run away or come to life in perfect form and try to kill him, naturally. Magicians are afraid of us!

WOULD YOU HAVE COME TO LIFE AND TRIED TO KILL HIM HAD HE MADE YOU PERFECTLY?

Probably. Are we done?

CHAPTER

3

As we continued to walk, the images changed to silver.

THE SILVER LIGHT DENOTES THE OLD KINGDOM, EGYPT'S FIRST GREAT AGE.

I saw armies clashing--Egyptians in kilts and sandals and leather armor, fighting with spears.

A tall, dark-skinned man in red-and-white armor placed a double crown on his head: **Narmer,** the king who united upper and lower Egypt.

Another few steps, and the images turned from silver to copper.

HERE WE ENTER THE MIDDLE KINGDOM. IT WAS A BLOODY, CHAOTIC TIME. AND YET THIS IS WHEN THE HOUSE OF LIFE CAME TO MATURITY.

The scenes shifted more rapidly. Every step covered hundreds of years, and yet the hall still went on forever.

Hatshepsut, the greatest female pharaoh, putting on a fake beard and ruling Egypt as a man.

Ramesses the Great leading his chariots into battle.

I saw a man with a fuzzy gray beard.

THIS MUST BE THE NEW KINGDOM! THE LAST TIME EGYPT WAS RULED BY EGYPTIANS.

IS THAT--

YOUR PEOPLE CALL HIM MOSES. THE ONLY FOREIGNE EVER TO DEFEAT THE HOUSE IN A MAGIC DUEL.

Workers building pyramids sprang up with each step we took.

Ten thousand workers gathered at its base and knelt before the pharaoh, who raised his hands to the sun, dedicating his own tomb.

I recognized his face from one of Dad's books.

THAT MUST BE KHUFU!

KHUFU THE BABOON?

NO SADIE, KHUFU THE PHARAOH. HE BUILT THE GREAT PYRAMID. IT WAS THE TALLEST STRUCTURE IN THE WORLD FOR ALMOST FOUR THOUSAND YEARS.

As we passed into a bronze gallery, I watched scenes passing that my dad had described to me.

For the first time, I understood just how ancient Egypt was.

THE NEW KINGDOM ENDED WHEN EGYPT'S LAST NATIVE-BORN PHARAOH, NECTANEBO II, WAS FORCED TO FLEE HIS POST BY PERSIAN INVADERS.

THE PTOLEMAIC PERIOD BEGAN AFTER ALEXANDER THE GREAT CONQUERED THE KNOWN WORLD, INCLUDING EGYPT.

HE SET UP HIS GENERAL PTOLEMY AS THE NEW LEADER, AND FOUNDED A LINE OF GREEK KINGS TO RULE OVER EGYPT.

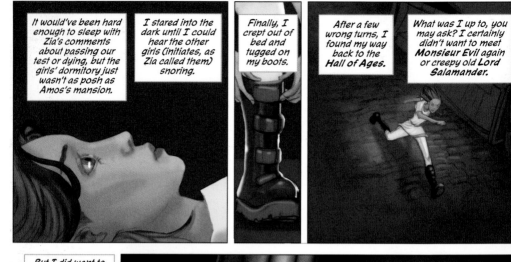

It would've been hard enough to sleep with Zia's comments about passing our test or dying, but the girls' dormitory just wasn't as posh as Amos's mansion.

I stared into the dark until I could hear the other girls (initiates, as Zia called them) snoring.

Finally, I crept out of bed and tugged on my boots.

After a few wrong turns, I found my way back to the Hall of Ages.

What was I up to, you may ask? I certainly didn't want to meet Monsieur Evil again or creepy old Lord Salamander.

But I did want to see those images-- memories, Zia had called them.

Zia had warned that the scenes would melt my brain, but I had a feeling she was just trying to scare me off. I felt a connection to those images, like there was an answer within-- a vital piece of information I needed.

I wanted another look at the Age of the Gods. A single leap, and I was there...

...in the Palace of the Gods.

MY LORD OSIRIS, HAPPY BIRTHDAY.

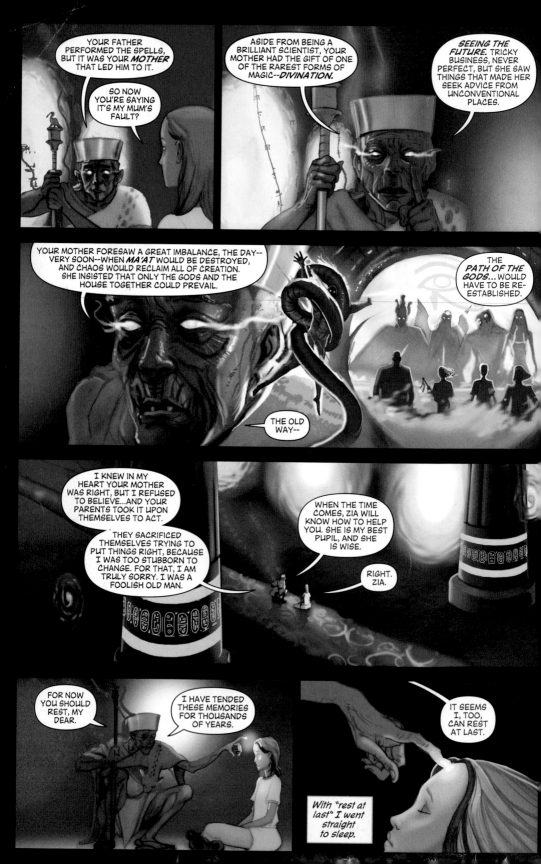

Inside the temple, two circles were drawn in the sand.

CARTER, SADIE, WE WILL BEGIN WITH A TEST OF YOUR MAGIC.

PLEASE TAKE A CIRCLE.

THE DUEL WILL START SLOWLY.

WAIT-- *DUEL?*

YES, A DUEL. GENERALLY SPEAKING, THE WAND IS FOR DEFENSE, THE STAFF IS FOR OFFENSE.

THE FIRST MAGICIAN TO KNOCK THE OTHER OUT OF HIS OR HER CIRCLE WINS.

BUT--WE HAVEN'T BEEN TRAINED!

THIS IS NOT SCHOOL, SADIE. YOU CANNOT LEARN MAGIC BY SITTING AT A DESK AND TAKING NOTES. YOU CAN ONLY LEARN MAGIC BY DOING MAGIC.

SUMMON WHATEVER POWER YOU CAN. USE WHATEVER YOU HAVE AVAILABLE. BEGIN!

OFFENSE, HUH?

I pulled something rodlike out of my satchel.

WHOA!

Immediately, the rod expanded until I was holding a two-meter-long staff!

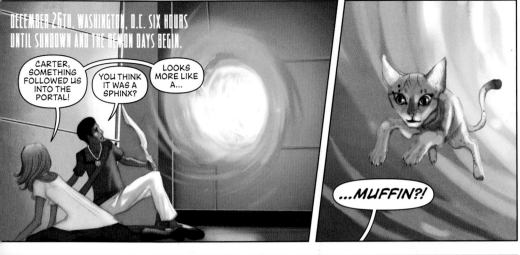

CARTER, SOMETHING FOLLOWED US INTO THE PORTAL!

YOU THINK IT WAS A SPHINX?

LOOKS MORE LIKE A...

...MUFFIN?!

BAST!

MISS ME?

EXCELLENT WORK WITH THE PORTAL, SADIE.

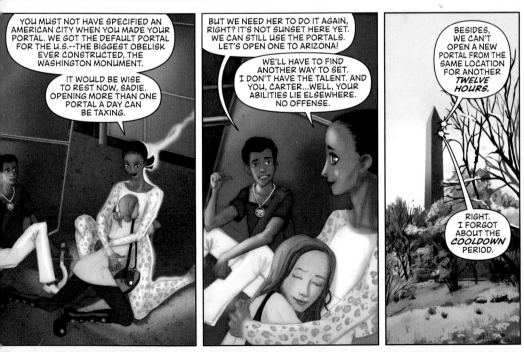

YOU MUST NOT HAVE SPECIFIED AN AMERICAN CITY WHEN YOU MADE YOUR PORTAL. WE GOT THE DEFAULT PORTAL FOR THE U.S.--THE BIGGEST OBELISK EVER CONSTRUCTED, THE WASHINGTON MONUMENT.

IT WOULD BE WISE TO REST NOW, SADIE. OPENING MORE THAN ONE PORTAL A DAY CAN BE TAXING.

BUT WE NEED HER TO DO IT AGAIN, RIGHT? IT'S NOT SUNSET HERE YET. WE CAN STILL USE THE PORTALS. LET'S OPEN ONE TO ARIZONA!

WE'LL HAVE TO FIND ANOTHER WAY TO GET. I DON'T HAVE THE TALENT. AND YOU, CARTER...WELL, YOUR ABILITIES LIE ELSEWHERE. NO OFFENSE.

BESIDES, WE CAN'T OPEN A NEW PORTAL FROM THE SAME LOCATION FOR ANOTHER *TWELVE HOURS.*

RIGHT. I FORGOT ABOUT THE *COOLDOWN* PERIOD.

I lay down to sleep, but my soul--my ba--had other ideas.

Carter had explained how his ba had left his body while he slept, but having it happen to me was another thing altogether!

It might have been fine for Carter to go about as a glowing turkey, but I have standards.

I concentrated hard, imagining my normal appearance (well, perhaps my appearance as I'd like it to be).

And voilà, my ba morphed into a human form--still see-through and glowing, mind you, but more like a proper ghost. And I had company!

HELLO, SADIE.

YOU'RE THE NUT!

I MEAN... THE SKY GODDESS.

SEEK OUT THOTH. HE HAS FOUND A NEW HOME IN MEMPHIS. HE CAN ADVISE YOU.

BE WARY, THOUGH: THOTH OFTEN ASKS FOR FAVORS, AND HE IS SOMETIMES HARD TO PREDICT.

AS GODDESS OF THE SKY, I CAN GUARANTEE YOU SAFE AIR TRAVEL AS FAR AS MEMPHIS. AS YOU GET CLOSER TO SET, YOU WILL BE BEYOND MY HELP. AND I CANNOT PROTECT YOU ON THE GROUND.

SEND MY SPIRIT BACK, THEN!

NOT YET. I HAD FIVE CHILDREN DURING THE DEMON DAYS. IF YOUR FATHER RELEASED ALL OF THEM, YOU SHOULD CONSIDER: WHERE IS THE FIFTH?

YOU MEAN NEPHTHYS, SET'S WIFE?

LASTLY... A FAVOR. IF YOU SEE MY HUSBAND GEB, WILL YOU GIVE HIM THIS?

IT'S THE LEAST I CAN DO. NOW, ABOUT SENDING ME BACK...

GODSPEED, SADIE KANE.

SADIE! YOU'RE AWAKE!

Reagan National was so close, I could see the planes landing across the Potomac.

The hard part was remembering what I was doing. I knew I was supposed to fly straight to the airport, but I kept getting distracted. Sadie must have been having the same problem, because I saw her veer off course to chase a squirrel. I forced myself to fly next to her and get her attention.

IT TAKES *WILLPOWER* TO STAY HUMAN. THE MORE TIME YOU SPEND AS A BIRD OF PREY, THE MORE YOU *THINK* LIKE ONE.

HA! HA! HA!

NOW YOU TELL ME.

I COULD *HELP.* GIVE ME CONTROL.

NOT TODAY, *BIRD-HEAD.*

We landed in the airport parking lot.

DECEMBER 27TH.
CAMELBACK MOUNTAIN,
PHOENIX, ARIZONA

OUR ENEMIES
ARE MORE
RESOURCEFUL
THAN I
IMAGINED.

THEY HAVE DISABLED MY
FAVORITE PET AND ARE NOW
FLYING UNDER THE PROTECTION
OF MOTHER NUT. WE MUST
BE DONE BEFORE
THEY ARRIVE...

WE WILL FINISH
CONSTRUCTION AT
SUNRISE ON YOUR
BIRTHDAY, MASTER!
I CONJURED A HUNDRED
MORE DEMONS TODAY
TO BOOST THE
WORKFORCE.

EXCELLENT.
THE DAWN OF MY NEW
KINGDOM IS IMMINENT!
I WILL SCOUR ALL LIFE
FROM THIS CONTINENT, AND
THIS PYRAMID WILL STAND
AS A MONUMENT TO MY
POWER--THE FINAL
TOMB OF OSIRIS!

YES, LORD!
BUT MIGHT
I ASK...

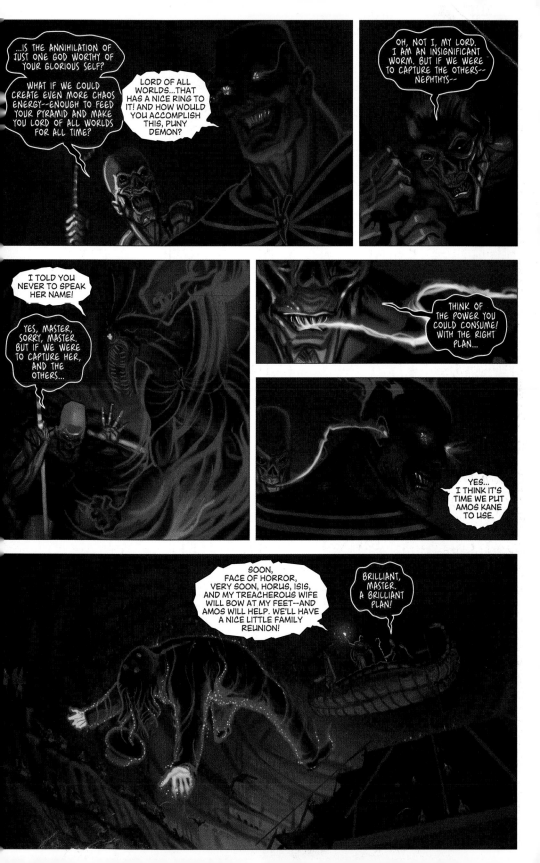

**DECEMBER 27TH.
MEMPHIS, TENNESSEE.
OSIRIS'S BIRTHDAY.**

Memphis hadn't gotten word that it was winter. The trees were green and the sky was a brilliant blue.

I managed to change back to human form on the plane. I'd done it by imagining Mum alive, us walking down Oxford Street together, gazing in the shop windows and talking and laughing--the kind of ordinary day we'd never gotten to share. An impossible wish, I know. But it had been powerful enough to remind me of who I was.

CHAPTER

5

We'd insisted Bast not "borrow" a car this time, so she agreed to rent one as long as we got a convertible. I didn't ask where she got the money, but soon we were cruising through the mostly deserted streets of Memphis with our BMW's top down.

IF I KNOW THOTH, HE'LL FIND A CENTER OF LEARNING. A LIBRARY, PERHAPS, OR A CACHE OF BOOKS IN A MAGICIAN'S TOMB.

MAYBE WE COULD TRY THE UNIVERSITY OF MEMPHIS? DAD DID A TALK THERE ONE TIME. IT SHOULD BE PRETTY CLOSE.

A few minutes later, we were strolling through the campus of a small college. It was eerily quiet, except for the sound of a ball echoing on concrete.

BABOONS. THE SACRED ANIMAL OF THOTH. WE MUST BE IN THE RIGHT PLACE.

We passed by athletic fields, and spotted five players in the middle of an intense game of pickup basketball.

IS THAT... A *LAKERS* JERSEY?

KHUFU!

AGH!

KHUFU SAYS YOU SMELL LIKE FLAMINGOS.

AGH!

YOU SPEAK *BABOONESE?*

ASK HIM WHERE HE'S BEEN ALL THIS TIME!

HORUS, *ISIS.* I SEE YOU'VE FOUND NEW BODIES.

UM, WE'RE NOT--

OH, I SEE. TRYING TO *SHARE THE BODY,* EH? DON'T THINK I'M FOOLED FOR A MINUTE, *ISIS!* I KNOW YOU'RE IN CHARGE.

WE'RE CARTER AND SADIE KANE. YOU'RE THOTH, I TAKE IT?

THAT'S WHAT THE GREEKS CALLED ME. MY EGYPTIAN NAME IS DJEHUTI. ALSO CALLED--

JAHOOTY?

I *ASSURE* YOU, IN ANCIENT EGYPTIAN IT'S A PERFECTLY FINE NAME.

WHAT CAN I *HELP* YOU WITH TODAY?

NUT TOLD US YOU COULD HELP US DEFEAT *SET.*

YOU HAVE THE *NERVE* TO ASK FOR HELP AFTER THE LAST TIME?

HUH? LAST TIME?

YES, LAST TIME! TO AVENGE HIS FATHER OSIRIS'S MURDER, *HORUS* CHALLENGED SET TO A DUEL. THE WINNER WOULD BECOME KING OF THE GODS.

THE BATTLE ALMOST DESTROYED THE WORLD, WHICH PUT ME IN A SPOT OF TROUBLE BECAUSE ONE OF MY *JOBS* IS TO MAINTAIN THE BALANCE *BETWEEN* ORDER AND CHAOS.

IT COULDN'T HAVE BEEN *THAT* BAD.

SET STABBED OUT HORUS'S EYE!

OUCH.

YES, AND I REPLACED IT WITH A NEW EYE MADE OF MOONLIGHT. THE EYE OF HORUS-- YOUR FAMOUS SYMBOL.

YOU MAY BE *BLOOD OF THE PHARAOHS,* BUT HORUS IS *RECKLESS.* AND AS FOR ISIS, WELL--

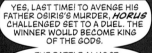

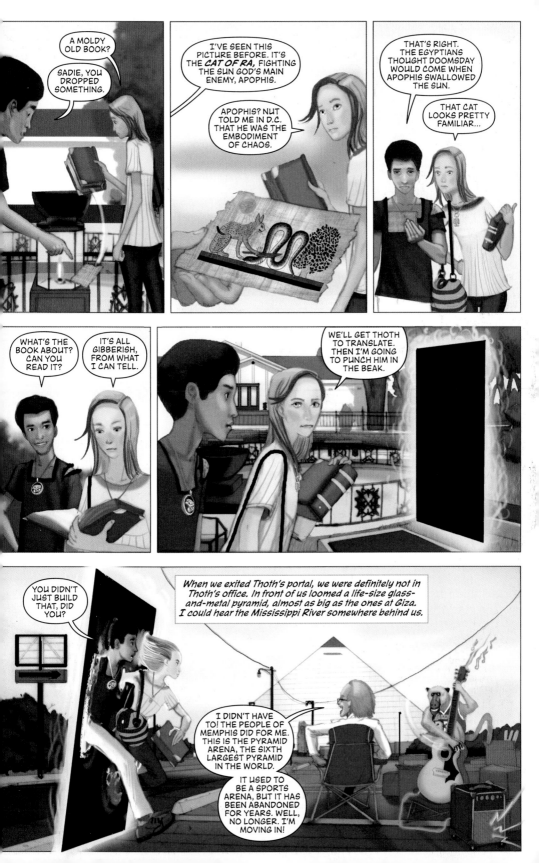

As far as rides to the land of death go, the boat was pretty cool. It was an old-time paddle steamboat with the name "Egyptian Queen" emblazoned on the side.

Bast was waiting for us at the gangplank.

CHILDREN, WELCOME ABOARD!

I CAN'T SAY I'M GLAD TO BE ON THIS BOAT AGAIN. I HATE THE WATER, BUT I SUPPOSE--

YOU'VE BEEN ON THIS BOAT BEFORE?

A MILLION QUESTIONS, AS USUAL. COME, YOU MUST MEET THE CAPTAIN.

The captain was waiting for us in the boat's wheelhouse.

LORD AND LADY KANE, IT IS AN HONOR TO HAVE YOU ABOARD.

I AM BLOODSTAINED BLADE. WHAT ARE YOUR ORDERS?

YOU TAKE ORDERS FROM US?

OF COURSE. THIS VESSEL, AND MY SERVICE, ARE BOUND TO YOUR FAMILY. WE CAN ONLY BE SUMMONED ONCE A YEAR, AND ONLY IN TIMES OF GREAT NEED.

WELL, IN THAT CASE, CAPTAIN VERY LARGE BLADE, OR WHATEVER IT IS, I ORDER YOU TO TAKE US TO THE LAND OF THE DEAD!

"OVER THE EONS IT BECAME CLEAR TO ME THAT RA'S PLAN WAS FOR THE SERPENT AND ME TO RIP EACH OTHER TO NOTHINGNESS.

"IT WAS MY DUTY... AND YET, WHEN YOUR PARENTS CAME ALONG..."

THEY GAVE YOU AN ESCAPE ROUTE, AND YOU TOOK IT.

YOUR FATHER SAID IT WAS THE FIRST STEP IN RESTORING THE GODS. I WAS RELIEVED TO TAKE HIS OFFER, BUT IT DOES NOT CHANGE THE FACT THAT I WAS A COWARD. I FAILED IN MY DUTY.

I AM THE QUEEN OF CATS. I HAVE MANY STRENGTHS. BUT TO BE HONEST...CATS ARE NOT VERY BRAVE.

Bast's story made me feel a bit guilty. According to Thoth, Isis had caused Ra to retreat into the heavens.

So in a ridiculous, maddening way, Bast's imprisonment had been my fault. I wanted to punch myself to get even with Isis, but I suspected it would hurt.

Our dinner conversation was cut short by rough waters and a call from the Captain.

ALL HANDS ON DECK!

Darkness swallowed the horizon, and along the riverbanks, the lights of towns changed to flickering fires, then winked out completely.

WE'RE COMING UPON THE *FIRST CATARACT!*

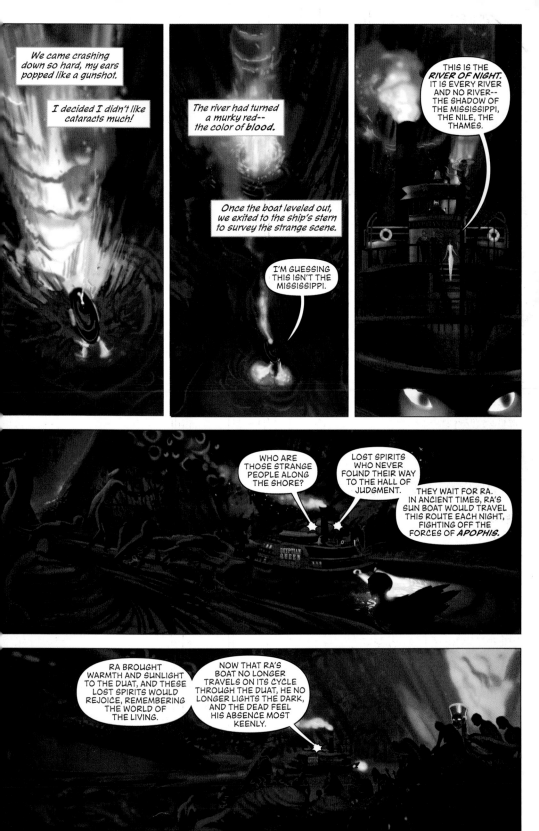

As our boat rounded a bend in the river, it opened up into a burning lake that stunk of burning petrol and rotten meat.

Through the shimmering heat, I could just make out an island in the middle of the lake. On it rose a glittering black temple that looked not at all friendly.

THE *LAKE OF FIRE!* WE'RE APPROACHING OUR DESTINATION.

I HOPE TO SEE YOU AGAIN, LORD AND LADY KANE.

YOUR CABINS WILL BE WAITING ABOARD THE *EGYPTIAN QUEEN.*

THANKS FOR EVERYTHING, AND, UH...STAY SHARP!

Instead of sailing away, the Egyptian Queen *simply* sank into the lava.

"STAY SHARP"?

I THOUGHT IT WAS FUNNY.

COME ALONG, CHILDREN. OUR BUSINESS LIES INSIDE THE TEMPLE.

Sniff Sniff BE ALERT. HE'S CLOSE.

WHO?

THE DOG.

Deep in the temple we found a large circular chamber. The center of the room was dominated by a set of broken scales.

WELCOME TO THE LAST ROOM YOU WILL EVER SEE.

THE HALL OF JUDGMENT WAS ONCE A CENTER OF MA'AT, BUT WITHOUT OSIRIS SEATED AT HIS THRONE, IT IS FALLEN INTO RUINS.

I spotted a strange figure at the base of the scales.

IS THAT--

AMMIT THE DEVOURER. LOOK UPON HIM AND TREMBLE.

I ALWAYS IMAGINED HIM... BIGGER.

We left New Orleans at 1:00 a.m. on December 28th with about twenty-four hours until Set planned to destroy the world. Nut had promised us safe travel only to Memphis, so we decided it'd be best to drive the rest of the way.

Bast "borrowed" a F.E.M.A. trailer from Hurricane Katrina. With luck, we'd get to Phoenix just in time to challenge Set. As for the House of Life, all we could do was hope to avoid them while we did our job.

Thoth

Land of the Dead

Bast and Khufu took turns driving while Sadie and I dozed off and on. I didn't know baboons could drive recreational vehicles, but Khufu did okay.

FEMA

CHAPTER

6

The guy was twenty feet tall--and I don't mean with a glowing avatar. He was all flesh and blood. If that wasn't weird enough, he appeared to be sweating at an unbelievable rate--oily water poured off him in torrents and pooled in the river.

I was conscious of Khufu nearby, trying to get Sadie out of harm's way. I had to keep this green guy distracted, at least until they were safe.

THAT FORM DOES NOT SERVE YOU, FALCON GOD. I WILL SNAP YOU IN HALF.

SOBEK?! YOUR DUTY IS TO THE KING!

WHAT KING? RA IS GONE. OSIRIS IS DEAD AGAIN, THE WEAKLING! AND HORUS CANNOT RESTORE THE EMPIRE WITH THIS BOY AS HIS HOST!

WHAT BRINGS YOU TO MY REALM, CAT GODDESS?

I THOUGHT YOU DIDN'T LIKE THE WATER!

CARTER, I WILL FINISH SOBEK. GO-- GET SADIE TO SAFETY!

My avatar form had protected me, but the impact had extinguished it.

BUT-- I CAN'T LEAVE YOU HERE ALONE!

GO! AND TELL YOUR FATHER I KEPT MY PROMISE.

Bast leaped at Sobek. The two grappled--Bast slashing furiously across his face while Sobek howled in pain. The two gods toppled into the water, and down they went.

Khufu and I stared at the spot where Sobek and Bast had gone under.

BAST-- NO!

The river bubbled and frothed violently. I could only guess what kind of fight was going on beneath the surface.

Amos flew us to White Sands,
New Mexico. He said it used to be
a government range for testing
missiles, and due to its remote
location, very unlikely anyone
would look for us there.

CHAPTER

7

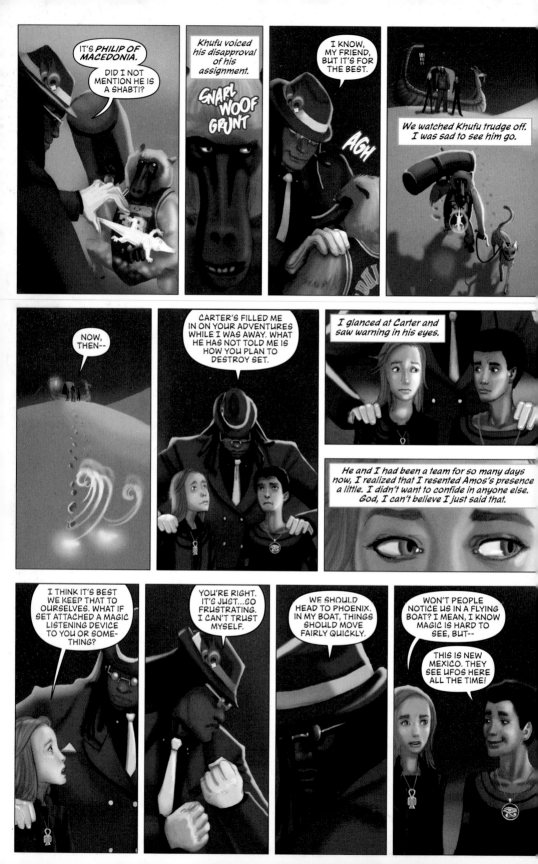

We were just packing the boat when a familiar voice pierced the desert night.

KANE!

DESJARDINS, ZIA RASHID, IT'S BEEN SEVERAL YEARS. I SEE ISKANDAR SENT HIS BEST.

ISKANDAR IS *DEAD*!

BAD NEWS, THEN...THAT MEANS...

HMM... IT APPEARS WE'VE BEEN TRACKED.

I AM THE *NEW CHIEF LECTOR*!

STEP OFF, MICHEL. FIGHTING US WILL GET YOU NOWHERE. WE MUST STOP SET. IF YOU'RE WISE--

I WOULD WHAT? JOIN YOU? COLLABORATE? THE GODS BRING NOTHING BUT DESTRUCTION.

MASTER, AMOS IS RIGHT. WE CAN'T FIGHT EACH OTHER. THAT'S NOT WHAT ISKANDAR WANTED.

YOU SIDE WITH *THEM*?

WE'RE HIT!

I steered the boat into a dive, scanning the landscape below us, but there was nowhere safe to land-- just subdivisions and office parks.

My more immediate concern was the unstoppable killing machine on our tail.

Seconds before impact with a well-lit factory complex, I had an idea.

CARTER, WHAT ARE YOU DOING! WE'RE GOING TO HIT ONE OF THOSE SILOS!

We reached Phoenix at half past four in the morning.

Less than a mile from Camelback Mountain, we entered a circle of perfect calm.

EYE OF THE STORM.

NOTHING'S MOVING ON THE STREETS. IF WE TRY TO DRIVE UP TO THE MOUNTAIN, WE'LL BE SEEN.

CHAPTER

8

WELL, NO ONE WILL NOTICE A FEW EXTRA WISPS OF BLACK CLOUD.

A STORM? THAT IS CHAOS MAGIC. WE SHOULD NOT--

With a poof poof poof we were all storm clouds.

Against our will, I might add.

I got so angry, a flash of lightning crackled inside me.

DON'T BE THAT WAY. IT'S ONLY FOR A FEW MINUTES. FOLLOW ME.

The mountain had an irresistible pull for my storm self. It glowed with heat, pressure, and turbulence--everything a little dust devil like me could want.

I followed Amos to a ridge on the side of the mountain, but I returned to human form a little too soon. I tumbled out of the sky and knocked Sadie to the ground.

OUCH!

SORRY!

ONLY THE PYRAMIDION LEFT.

THE WHAT? LET ME SEE.

Every move was perfect.

YOU CAN DIE KNOWING YOU MADE A GOOD EFFORT, HORUS, BUT IT'S MUCH TOO LATE.

LOOK!

The House of Life must've gathered all its forces, but they were pathetically few against Set's legions.

Magician after magician was completely overwhelmed, going down under the enemy wave.

THIS IS THE END OF THE HOUSE! THEY CANNOT PREVAIL AS LONG AS MY PYRAMID STANDS!

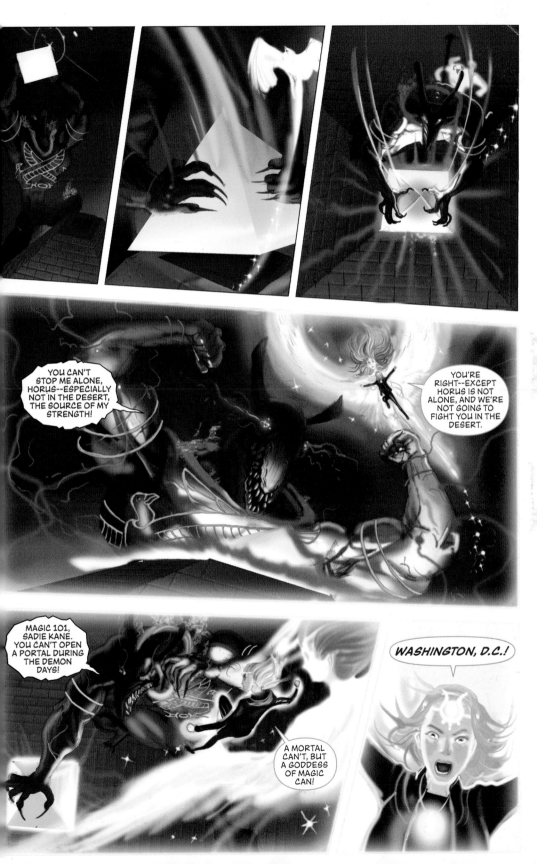

DIE!

EEP!

THIS IS NOT OVER, GODLING. ALL THIS I HAVE WROUGHT WITH A WISP OF MY VOICE, THE MEREST BIT OF MY ESSENCE WRIGGLING.

IMAGINE WHAT I SHALL DO WHEN... FULLY... FORMED...

APOPHIS'S VOICE POSSESSED FACE OF HORROR. HE WAS USING YOU TO SERVE HIS PURPOSE ALL ALONG, SET,

RIDICULOUS! THE SNAKE IN THE CLOUDS WAS ONE OF YOUR TRICKS, ISIS. AN *ILLUSION*.

LOOK, CARTER!

THAT LIGHT-- IT'S JUST LIKE THE SHABTI IN MEMPHIS!

REMEMBER WHAT THOTH SAID? "SHABTI MAKE EXCELLENT STUNT DOUBLES." THAT'S WHAT SHE WAS.

ISKANDAR MUST'VE HIDDEN THE REAL ZIA...

HE KNEW SHE'D BE IN DANGER WHEN THE SPIRIT OF NEPHTHYS JOINED WITH HER IN *LONDON!*

THEN... THE REAL ZIA IS ALIVE...

...AND THAT BLUE LIGHT'S PROBABLY REPORTING *BACK* TO HER! WE SHOULD *TRACK* IT!

CARTER, I'M NOT SURE IF NOW'S THE BEST TIME.

WE'RE PRACTICALLY IN THE PRESIDENT'S BACKYARD.

IF WE DON'T GET OUT OF D.C. SOON, WE'RE GOING TO HAVE TO ANSWER TO SOME HEAVILY ARMED COMPANY!

The evening news would eventually attribute our adventures to a rare occurrence of the northern lights. But all the cameras could show was a big square of melted snow on the mall, which kind of made for boring video.

We managed to escape the cameras, and the police. I had just enough magic to turn myself into a falcon and Amos into... a hamster. (Hey, I was rushed!)

We headed back to the mansion, since we had nowhere else to go.

EPILOGUE

We had managed to save the world, but we couldn't help feeling a little defeated.

The mansion was in a terrible state from being blown up, and we'd failed to save our dad.

Carter'd lost his first girlfriend, and Amos was suffering the effects of post-traumatic Set disorder.

It took Sadie and I several weeks to make the house livable again. We used magic, but it was a lot harder without Isis or Horus to help.

Amos was the worse for wear. He'd been taken over by Set, his will broken. I wondered if he'd ever be the same.

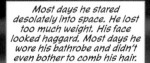

Most days he stared desolately into space. He lost too much weight. His face looked haggard. Most days he wore his bathrobe and didn't even bother to comb his hair.

We stowed Isis's and Horus's amulets in a box in the library.

Eventually we got the walls and ceilings repaired, and cleaned up the debris until the house no longer smelled of smoke. Every day, I went to sleep feeling as if I'd done twelve hours of hard labor.

I'VE BROUGHT YOU HERE TO TELL YOU BOTH HOW PROUD I AM OF YOU. THE GODS ARE VERY MUCH IN YOUR DEBT.

BUT WHAT *ARE* YOU? MY DAD? OSIRIS? ARE YOU EVEN *ALIVE*?

I AM BOTH OSIRIS AND JULIUS KANE.

I AM ALIVE AND DEAD, THOUGH THE TERM *RECYCLED* IS CLOSER TO THE TRUTH.

Osiris is the god of the dead, and the god of new life. To return him to his throne--

YOU HAD TO *DIE.* YOU KNEW THIS GOING INTO IT. YOU INTENTIONALLY HOSTED OSIRIS, KNOWING YOU WOULD DIE. *THIS* IS WHAT YOU MEANT BY "MAKING THINGS RIGHT"?

CARTER, WHEN OSIRIS WAS ALIVE, HE WAS A GREAT KING. BUT WHEN HE *DIED*--

HE BECAME A THOUSAND TIMES MORE POWERFUL.

IF THERE IS CHAOS HERE IN THE DUAT, IT REVERBERATES IN THE UPPER WORLD. HELPING OSIRIS TO HIS THRONE WILL BRING ORDER BACK TO THE DUAT.

MY DUTIES HERE ARE MORE IMPORTANT THAN ANYTHING I COULD HAVE DONE IN THE WORLD ABOVE-- EXCEPT BEING YOUR FATHER. AND I AM STILL YOUR FATHER.

THERE IS ANOTHER REASON I MADE MY CHOICE, AS YOU CAN PROBABLY GUESS.

Just when things were settling down to a nice safe routine, Sadie and I decided to embark on our new mission.

I'M SORRY, GRAN, BUT I'M AFRAID I CAN'T COME HOME TO LONDON. YES, I'LL BE SURE TO VISIT, BUT I'M REALLY NEEDED HERE.

LOVE YOU TOO, GRAN. BYE!

CARTER, WHAT ARE YOU WEARING?

YOU LOOK ALMOST LIKE A REGULAR TEENAGER!

IT'S, UM, ALL COTTON. OKAY FOR MAGIC. DAD WOULD PROBABLY THINK I LOOK LIKE A GANGSTER...

DAD WOULD THINK YOU LOOK LIKE AN IMPECCABLE MAGICIAN, BECAUSE THAT'S WHAT YOU ARE.

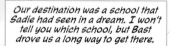

NOW, COME ON. OUR MISSION AWAITS!

Our destination was a school that Sadie had seen in a dream. I won't tell you which school, but Bast drove us a long way to get there.

Several times, the forces of chaos tried to stop us. Several times, we heard rumors that our enemies were starting to hunt down other descendants of the pharaohs, trying to thwart our plans.

Now we're back at the Twenty-first Nome in Brooklyn.

Our parents promised to see us again, so we'll have to return to the Land of the Dead eventually, which I think is fine with Sadie, as long as Anubis is there.

Zia is out there somewhere-- the real Zia. I intend to find her.

The Kane family has a lot of work to do, and so do you.

If this story falls into your hands, there's probably a reason. Look for the djed. It won't take much to awaken your power.

Maybe you'll want to follow the path of Horus or Isis, Thoth or Anubis, or even Bast. Whatever you decide, the House of Life needs new blood if we're going to survive.

Most of all, chaos is rising. Apophis is gaining strength, which means we have to gain strength too--gods and men, united as in olden times. It's the only way the world won't be destroyed.

Adapted from the novel
The Kane Chronicles, Book One: *The Red Pyramid*

Text copyright © 2012 by Rick Riordan
Illustrations copyright © 2012 Disney Enterprises, Inc.

Design by Jim Titus

Printed in the United States of America
V381-8386-5-12197

First graphic novel edition
10 9 8 7 6 5 4 3 2 1

ISBN 978-1-4231-5068-8 (hardcover)
ISBN 978-1-4231-5069-5 (paperback)

The red pyramid : the graphic novel / Rick Riordan ; adapted by
Orpheus Collar ; lettered by Jared Fletcher. —1st ed.
     p. cm.
     "Adapted from the novel The Kane Chronicles, Book One: The Red Pyramid."
     Summary: Brilliant Egyptologist Dr. Julius Kane accidentally unleashes
the Egyptian god Set, who banishes the doctor to oblivion and forces his two
children to embark on a dangerous journey, bringing them closer to the truth
about their family and its links to a secret order that has existed since the time
of the pharaohs.
     1. Graphic novels. [1. Graphic novels. 2. Adventure and
adventurers—Fiction. 3. Voyages and travels—Fiction. 4. Mythology,
Egyptian—Fiction. 5. Magic—Fiction. 6. Brothers and sisters—Fiction.
7. Secrets—Fiction. 8. Riordan, Rick. Red pyramid—Adaptations.] I.
Riordan, Rick. Red pyramid. II. Title.
     PZ7.7.C647Red 2012
     741.5'973—dc23
                         2012007905

Visit www.disneyhyperionbooks.com